Aschenputtel
&
The Light Princess

Aschenputtel & The Light Princess

Fairytales Retold
Double Edition

Avril Sabine

Cracked Acorn

Productions
Australia

Aschenputtel & The Light Princess

Fairytales Retold Double Edition

Published by

Cracked Acorn Productions

PO Box 1365

Gympie, Queensland 4570

Australia

978-1-925131-56-7 (Large Type Print)

Genre: Fairytales Retold Short Story

Copyright 2016 © Avril Sabine

Cover design by Caitlyn Petersen

Aschenputtel

*

The Light Princess

Aschenputtel

When Aschenputtel's mother dies, her father marries a woman with two daughters of her own. They treat her like a servant and she's left to sleep on the hearth amongst the ashes, her only friend a little bird that nests in the hazel tree, which grew at her mother's grave. When the king throws a feast to find his son a bride, Aschenputtel begs to attend. Her family answers her with taunts and impossible tasks. She's determined to complete them so she can attend the feast.

*

People have been telling stories since the beginning of time. Fairytales, folklore, myths and legends are among some of the stories that have been told over and over through the centuries. The basic story remains the same, but each storyteller adds their own style, sometimes adding something unique to the tale.

*

This story was written by an Australian author using Australian spelling.

Aschenputtel

Aschenputtel knelt in front of her mother's grave where she was buried in the garden, pressing a hazel twig into the dirt. Tears ran down her face, splashed onto her hands and dampened the earth around the twig. She closed her eyes. It hadn't meant anything to him. She'd felt certain when she'd asked Claude, her father, for the first twig that brushed against his hat after he turned for home, he would remember his first wife. She'd always asked him to bring her that first twig. When he'd returned from the fair, with the gifts they'd all asked for, the twig had seemed to mean no more to him than the fine clothes, pearls and diamonds her stepsisters had demanded.

"I miss you." Her words were a whisper, dragged from her even though she knew her stepsisters would torment her if they heard. Was her mother watching over her like she'd promised? If she was, how could she let that woman, her father had married, treat her the way she did? Like a servant, she was to fetch the water, light the fire, cook the meals and wash the clothes. She was not a servant. Her hands curled into fists. Yet when she complained, her father told her to behave and mind her manners and listen to her mother.

That woman wasn't her mother.

No, her mother lay buried and not even a year had passed before she'd been replaced. She reached out and pressed the dirt more firmly around the twig. She hadn't forgotten. Not one single thing. The image came clearly to her mind. Her mother smiling, kissing her husband goodbye and telling him to bring her the first twig that brushed against his hat after he turned for home. She'd expected something when she'd ask for the twig. Anything. But his expression had remained the same. Not even a hint of remembrance had clouded his gaze.

"Aschenputtel!"

She was tempted to ignore Jeanne, her stepmother, who stood at the back door. But that was never a good idea. The chores would be piled upon her until she had so much to do that even sleep would be denied her that night. Rising wearily to her feet, she walked towards the house.

"Do you hear me, you lazy girl? Get inside and start the evening meal. Must I do everything around here?"

Aschenputtel bit back the words she wanted to say. The only thing her stepmother seemed to do around here was order her about. Shoulders slumping, she made her way to the kitchen and began to prepare the meal. Life had been so different when her mother had been alive.

Once the meal was over, she'd eaten the scraps her stepmother allowed her and cleaned up the kitchen. She curled up on the hearth amongst the ashes, thinking of the bedroom she'd once slept in. There'd been a large timber bed with a soft feather mattress, crisp linen sheets and warm blankets. One of her stepsisters had it now. Justine, the oldest one. Yvonne had what had once been a guest room. It seemed an age ago. Back when she'd had another name, not one given to torment her. She shouldn't think about those years, should try and accept the way things were now. But it was impossible. Maybe if she hadn't known any different, she wouldn't yearn for all she'd lost. Still thinking about what life had been like when her mother had been alive, she fell asleep.

The days seemed to blend. Each feeling the same as the previous. She found herself working from dawn to late at night, escaping to her mother's grave several times a day. She tried not to, but tears flowed as she thought of how her family treated her. The hurtful words, the nasty pranks, the constant demands. As the months passed, the twig grew into a tree, watered by her bitter tears and the wish that her mother still lived.

One day, not long after her eighteenth birthday, Aschenputtel ran from the house, the sound of her stepsisters' laughter ringing out behind her. She threw herself at the base of the hazel tree that had grown at her mother's grave. What had she done to make them torment her like this? The tears she refused to let fall in front of them poured down her cheeks.

A small bird flew out of the tree to land in front of her. "What can I do to help you?"

Aschenputtel stared at the bird, trying to stop crying. "You can speak?"

The bird fluttered closer, jumping

across the ground. "Of course I can. Now tell me, what can I do to help?"

She looked from the bird to the tree. "Where did you come from?"

"I have a nest in the tree." He turned his head in the direction of the hazel tree.

Aschenputtel couldn't see the nest, but the leafy tree could have easily hidden a dozen nests amongst its branches. "How can you help me?" She was afraid no one could help.

"What do you want?"

Her gaze was drawn to the grave. The one thing she most wanted, she couldn't have. Her stomach rumbled, reminding her she hadn't been given food today. Jeanne had told her she didn't deserve anything with how lazy she'd been yesterday. She'd forgotten one thing from more than a dozen tasks she'd been set. It wasn't fair that she'd been punished over something so small. Not after the hours she'd worked. "Something to eat."

Without answering, the bird flew off.

Aschenputtel watched it go, not expecting to see it again. The day had nearly ended when the little bird returned, flying into the kitchen as she put away the dishes she'd washed. It landed on the table, placing berries on the scrubbed timber.

"Is there anything else I can do for you?"

She picked up the berries, popping one of them into her mouth. The sweet flavour had her wanting to cram them all in at once. It had been a long time since she'd tasted anything so delicious. "Thank you. These are wonderful." The kindness of the bird brought tears to her eyes.

"Would you like more berries?"

She nodded, her mouth full. Before she had a chance to speak, the bird took flight, leaving through the open window. She crossed the room and looked into the night, unable to see the little bird. Aschenputtel remained there as she ate the last of the berries. The house was quiet around her, the fire had nearly died out in the hearth and she felt exhausted after a day of being at Jeanne's beck and call. But for once, she didn't feel alone. She tried to remember the last time she'd had this feeling. It didn't take her long to figure it out. The last time had been before she'd lost her mother. With one last look for the bird, she turned away from the window and headed for the hearth where she curled up and fell asleep, her lips curving into a smile, the taste of berries a comforting memory.

Over the next few months the little bird brought Aschenputtel gifts. It regularly brought berries, nuts, seeds and flowers. Once it even brought a silk ribbon, dropping it into her hand as she sat under the hazel tree. She hid it in the tree, not wanting one of her stepsisters to steal it.

The many gifts and the company of the bird made life far more bearable and she sometimes found herself humming and smiling as she worked. It was while she was cleaning out the fireplace in the parlour, trying not to hum since Jeanne was sitting nearby reading, that she couldn't help wondering that she even remembered how to smile. She had very little to smile about. Other than her feathered friend.

Her stepsisters burst into the room, dragging her from her thoughts. Their colourful gowns made her think of flowers and sunshine, the scent of their perfumes as dainty and delicate as the two blue eyed, brown haired girls. How she wished she could have visited their friends with them. Wished that they didn't torment her and treat her like a servant.

"We heard the most delightful news," Yvonne said.

Justine turned on her sister with a glare. "I'm telling her." She faced her mother. "King Percevel is holding a feast that will last for three nights. Everyone is invited. Oh if only we'd learned about it earlier. We have nothing new to wear."

Yvonne stepped past her sister. "You haven't heard the best part yet. It's for his son, Prince Lucien. The king has decided it's time for him to take a bride."

Jeanne rose to her feet, letting the book close as she tossed it onto the chair. She smiled fondly at her daughters. "We must hurry. The prince is sure to want to marry one of you. No other lady hereabouts can hold a candle to your beauty."

Aschenputtel, still crouched in front of the fireplace, didn't doubt Jeanne's words. Her stepsisters were beautiful and had numerous suitors. The prince would be caught by their looks too. If only she could go. She stared at her hands, ash coating them. Who would let a dirty, poorly dressed girl attend a ball? Her heart sank as she watched her stepmother and stepsisters discuss what would be the best outfit for each of them. She wanted to escape to the garden, but hoped if she remained quiet and still they would ignore her.

"Aschenputtel! What are you doing, you lazy girl?" Jeanne brushed past her daughters to glare at Aschenputtel. "Go and clean the shoes. Hurry. We're running out of time." She spun on her heel and strode from the room, her daughters following her.

After Aschenputtel had cleaned the shoes and ran around completing the many tasks demanded of her, she couldn't resist asking Jeanne to let her go too.

Jeanne stared at her a moment before bursting out laughing. "You? Dressed as you are? You have nothing to wear and can't even dance. Why would you even want to go to the feast? You should thank me for saving you from the mockery of the guests."

Aschenputtel reached for Jeanne, but the woman stepped away, a look of disgust for the dirty hand stretched towards her. "Please. I don't need to dance, or even join in the feast. No one would have to know I was there. Please let me go." She couldn't stop pleading, no matter how much her stepsisters and Jeanne mocked her. This was her only chance to visit the castle. The king had one child so it wasn't likely he'd ever invite everyone to the castle for a feast again.

Eventually, Jeanne said, "You want to go to the feast?"

Aschenputtel nodded, hope starting to fill her. She clasped her hands in front of her to prevent herself from reaching for Jeanne again.

"Follow me." Jeanne strode to the kitchen, everyone trailing after her. Reaching the kitchen, she took a dishful of peas and tossed them into the ash heap. "If you can pick them out within two hours you may join us."

Aschenputtel stared at the scattered peas while her stepsisters laughed. The hope she'd felt, died.

"Come, girls. We need to finish getting ready." Jeanne swept from the room.

Fighting back tears, Aschenputtel raced outside to the hazel tree. Seeing it reminded her of her friend, the little bird. Maybe he and his friends could help her pick the peas from the ash. She called out to them. Turtle-doves, linnets, blackbirds, thrushes and chaffinches. They came to her, following her to the kitchen and picking the peas from the ash and dropping them into the dish. It took them less than an hour and they flew out the window the moment the job was complete.

Smiling, she gathered up the dish and went in search of Jeanne. She found her helping Justine finish dressing. Her smile faded when she saw her stepsister. The prince would want to dance all night with Justine. Aschenputtel had never seen her stepsister look so beautiful. She caught sight of herself in the mirror Justine stood near. She almost didn't recognise herself.

Once light brown hair with golden streaks was now the colour of the ashes from the fireplace. The rest of her was equally as dirty, including her drab, grey dress. The tears nearly welled up again. Forcing them down, she took another step into the room, holding out the peas, forcing herself to speak the name she always stumbled over. "Mother, I gathered the peas as you requested."

Jeanne gave her one of her usual looks of disgust. "You couldn't have. Somehow you must have cheated."

"No." Aschenputtel held the dish out further. "Look. These are the peas you threw in the hearth. They've all been collected."

Jeanne snatched the dish from her and strode to the kitchen where she took a second dish of peas. She threw both lots of peas into the ashes. "If you pick all the peas from the ashes in one hour you can go to the feast too."

Aschenputtel gaped as she watched Jeanne leave the dishes on the table and stride from the room, calling Justine to follow.

Justine remained in the doorway a moment longer, smirking. "How dare you even think you can attend the feast. Did you expect us to let you in the carriage with us? Father wouldn't want someone as dirty as you in our carriage." With a look of disgust, similar to the one her mother used, Justine left the kitchen.

Aschenputtel stared at the empty doorway. It had taken the birds nearly an hour to pick one dish of peas from the ashes. How could they pick two from them in the same amount of time? Weariness tugged at her. It would be far easier to curl up on the hearth and sleep rather than trying to find a way to attend the feast. She looked from the hearth to the door leading to the garden. Deciding to give it one more try, she walked to the hazel tree and called the birds like she had before. The sun had set and she feared that none would answer her call.

They came, nearly twice as many as before, and picked the peas from the ashes. They were done in half an hour and Aschenputtel gathered the two dishes, hurrying through the house looking for Jeanne. This time she found her helping Yvonne to finish getting ready.

Aschenputtel held out the two dishes. "I gathered all the peas as you requested, Mother." She stumbled on the last word.

"Look at yourself." Jeanne gestured towards her. "Would you go to the feast dressed like that?"

Aschenputtel looked down at herself. "I thought maybe I could borrow something from Justine or Yvonne." Her words were hesitant.

"You're not borrowing anything from me," Yvonne said. "I would have to burn it afterwards."

Jeanne turned to Yvonne. "Fetch your sister. Your father will be back with the carriage at any moment. We don't want to be late."

When Yvonne walked past her, keeping her skirts well away, Aschenputtel wanted to argue that he wasn't her stepsister's father. He was hers. But he hadn't really been hers since he'd remarried and acted like his first marriage hadn't existed. Including the child born of it.

Jeanne crossed the room, pausing in the doorway to send her a look of disgust. "Did you really think we'd let you shame us by attending the feast? You must be stupid as well as lazy."

She sailed from the room, head high, mocking laughter trailing behind her.

Aschenputtel nearly dropped the dishes of peas. All that kept her from letting go was the thought of having to clean them up later. Hearing the carriage pull up, she left the dishes in the kitchen before running to the parlour window.

Outside her father helped her stepsisters and Jeanne into the carriage, the carriage lanterns clearly showing the fond smile he gave his wife. Pain arrowed through Aschenputtel and she wanted to run out there and demand he take her too. Demand he not forget she existed. It was too late. He was already climbing into the carriage and the coachman was driving off into the night. The house was empty and she was alone again.

She ran to the hazel tree, tears streaming down her face, the light of the nearly full moon lighting her way. For once they weren't tears of sorrow. Anger coursed through her and she called out, "I wanted to go too." She repeated the words, quieter this time. "I wanted to go to the feast too."

The little bird flew out of the tree. "How can I help you?"

"I have nothing to wear. How can I attend the feast without a ball gown?" She thought of the dresses her stepsisters had worn, wanting one that would outshine them. "A dress of silver and gold. One that no one would recognise me in." She sighed, knowing she asked for the impossible. "I'm sorry. You must be tired of hearing all my complaints." Without answering the bird flew into the tree and Aschenputtel stared at the shadowy leaves he'd disappeared into. She guessed he was.

Before she could rise to her feet and return inside, the bird flew out of the tree with a silver and gold dress and slippers of spangled silk. Aschenputtel was afraid to touch them, worried she might soil them with her dirt. She gingerly carried them inside and washed the dirt from her body before donning the clothes and dressing her hair. Standing in front of Justine's mirror she once again barely recognised herself. The young woman reflected in the mirror was nothing like her usual self. Not a single person would recognise her. A smile slowly formed. Not even her father.

She raced through the house, hurrying through the streets to the castle, not wanting to miss too much of the feast. When she arrived, she was ushered inside and treated like royalty. Her smile grew wider when she heard some of the whispers as people speculated over who she was. Her favourite was that she must be a foreign princess.

The evening felt like a dream. The dress she wore was so much more than she'd ever owned and the food was delicious. She ate far less than what she would have liked for fear she'd be sick from the rich food. People smiled at her and spoke politely, treating her like she was someone important. She didn't want the evening to ever end. Didn't want to return to a life of drudgery and servitude.

When Prince Lucien came towards her, smiling, she nearly forgot to breathe. His black hair was neatly styled, his brown eyes stared straight at her, rather than through her like she was accustomed to, and his clothes were trimmed with gold. She dropped into a curtsey as he stopped in front of her. "Your Royal Highness." She was amazed her voice was steady when inside she quaked with terror that she might say or do something that would show him she was only a kitchen wench.

Lucien bowed to her, holding out his hand. "Will you do me the honour of dancing with me?"

Worried she would stumble and make a fool of herself, Aschenputtel took the hand he held out. "Could we take a walk in the gardens first? I've been told they're magnificent."

"Certainly."

They wandered through the

gardens, which were lit by coloured lanterns. At first Aschenputtel was nervous, uncertain how to answer Lucien's many questions. Eventually, she began to ask him questions of her own. The hours passed far too quickly and somehow she found herself agreeing to dance with him and they returned inside.

She didn't stumble once. The lessons she'd had while her mother had been alive slowly came back to her. When the dance ended, a gentleman stopped at her side and bowed. She dropped into a curtsey, not as deep as the one she'd offered Lucien.

"Would you do me the honour of dancing with me?"

Still holding onto Lucien's arm, she tried to think of a way to politely decline.

"The lady is dancing with me," Lucien said.

The gentleman bowed towards Lucien. "Of course, Your Royal Highness."

Aschenputtel smiled up at Lucien as they began to dance again. The night was like a dream. She'd never expected the prince to want to dance with her. Nor had she thought she'd have the chance to wander the gardens with him, talking half the night. All she'd originally hoped for was to be able to see the castle and the beautifully dressed people. To have a glimpse into their lives that were far removed from her own.

When some of the guests began to leave, Aschenputtel thought it best to go too. She didn't want her family to arrive home and find her gone. When the current dance ended, she drew away from Lucien. "I must leave. Thank you for such a wonderful evening." She spun from him, not wanting Lucien to see the tears gathering in her eyes.

"Wait," Lucien called out.

She didn't stop. Hurrying through the guests, she fled the ballroom. The last thing she wanted to do was burst into tears in front of all these people. The evening was over and she had to return to her life. There was no way the prince, or anyone for that matter, would be interested in her if they knew the truth. She reached the stairs outside the castle and stumbled, her slippers making it difficult to run.

"Wait. Please wait. I never even asked your name."

Ignoring Lucien's pleas, she ran into the night. He continued to follow her and not wanting him to know where she lived, she jumped up into the pigeon house at the back of her father's garden, begging the birds to help her escape. She went out the other side of the pigeon house and fled to the hazel tree where she returned her finery to the little bird.

Dressing in her dirty gown and messing up her hair, she coated her skin with the ashes from the hearth. Peeking out the back door, she could see the prince at the pigeon house looking for her. Shoulders slumping, she turned away and slowly walked to the hearth where she curled up. How was she ever going to endure her days now? She hadn't thought about that. An evening spent being treated like a princess made her crave an escape. But she had no idea how to escape from her father's home. Where could she go? How would she live? The sound of her family arriving home brought her thoughts to an end. She closed her eyes, pretending she was fast asleep.

It didn't take long for pretending to become reality and she fell asleep to dream about dancing with Lucien. Her dreams were interrupted by Jeanne's voice.

"You lazy girl, wake up. How dare you sleep half the day away? You think we should feed you when you can't even help around here?"

Aschenputtel staggered to her feet, surprised to find Jeanne was right. She'd slept the morning away. "I'm sorry." She ducked her head as she scurried away to make the morning meal.

By evening, she was ready to throw something at her stepsisters. Or at least tell them she'd been at the feast too. They'd spent the entire day telling her about all she'd supposedly missed out on and the mysterious princess Lucien had spent most of the evening with. When they finally left for the second night of the feast, Aschenputtel made her way to the hazel tree, anger burning through her. She would have one more night of being treated like a princess. Just one more night. Then she'd be able to return to her normal life.

Like the previous night, she asked the little bird to bring her clothes of silver and gold. He flew down out of the tree with a gown more magnificent than the previous one. As soon as she was washed and dressed, she hurried through the streets to the castle.

Lucien waited for her, taking her hand the moment she stepped into the ballroom. "Will you take a walk in the gardens with me?"

"I'd be honoured, Your Royal Highness." She took the hand he offered her and walked beside him.

"Please, call me Lucien."

She inclined her head.

"You never told me your name."

She couldn't give it to him, not without him learning who she was. There was no way she wanted him to learn she was a dirty, unwanted girl who slept in the ashes of the hearth at her father's home. She smiled up at him, thinking of the tree the little bird lived in. "Hazel."

They spent the night talking and dancing and when they joined the rest of the guests for the meal, Lucien asked her to sit at his side. It was as much of a dream as the previous night and she didn't want it to end.

Every time a gentleman asked her to dance with him, Lucien would tell them she was dancing with him and the second time he said it, she smiled up at him.

"You don't mind?"

She continued to smile at him. "No, not at all."

The night passed far too quickly and when guests started to leave, Aschenputtel drew away from Lucien. "I have to return home."

"Stay."

She shook her head. "No, I'm sorry, I must leave." She couldn't let her family arrive home before her and find her missing.

"Let me take you home in my carriage."

She started to argue, then thought it might be a way to slip away from him rather than have him chase her through the streets like the previous night. "I'll wait out the front."

As soon as she was out of Lucien's sight, she ran to the stairs and hurried down them. She was nearly home before she heard Lucien behind her, calling for her to wait. She sprang up into a large pear tree not far from the pigeon house, slipping out the other side of it and hurrying to the hazel tree where she returned the finery to the little bird.

By the time her family arrived home, she was once again in her dirty dress and covered in ash, curled up on the hearth and pretending to be asleep. She was starting to congratulate herself on her narrow escape when she heard Lucien's voice in the hallway. It took all her willpower not to run out and see what he was doing. She crept to the kitchen doorway so she could hear him more clearly.

"The lady I spent the night dancing with disappeared into the pear tree in your garden. Would you happen to know who she might be?"

"No, but let me fetch my axe and chop down the tree so we can all find out who she is," Claude said.

Aschenputtel hurried back to the hearth and curled up, half closing her eyes. She watched as her father and Lucien came through the kitchen, Jeanne, Justine and Yvonne trailing behind them. The two girls clutched at each other, giggling and whispering. Aschenputtel was glad Lucien didn't even spare them a glance.

Once they'd all trooped outside, she dashed across the room to peer out the door. Claude swung his axe at the pear tree as everyone watched. When it came crashing to the ground, he helped Lucien look amongst the branches. Aschenputtel was tempted to call out to Lucien when she saw the dejected slump of his shoulders as he bid them goodnight and walked away alone. Only the thought of what he'd think of her, dressed in her filthy gown and looking nothing like the glamorous woman he sought, kept her quiet.

Seeing her family were returning to the house, she crept back to her place at the hearth. When her stepsisters left the room, sent to bed by Jeanne, Aschenputtel was tempted to open her eyes to see why her parents remained in the kitchen.

"Who do you think she is?" Jeanne asked.

"I have no idea. For a moment I

thought it might be my daughter, but that was a stupid notion," Claude said.

Jeanne laughed. "That dirty, lazy girl? You foolish man, whatever could you have been thinking?"

Claude remained silent and Aschenputtel again fought the urge to open her eyes.

"I'm going to bed. We have a lot to do when we wake. Yesterday I had the girls' measurements sent to the dressmaker. They'll outshine that mysterious lady and catch the prince's attention. It's their last chance to make an impression."

Aschenputtel heard Jeanne's footsteps leave the room. She didn't hear Claude move. When she was about to finally open her eyes, she heard his footsteps. They brought him closer rather than further away. He stood in front of her and she couldn't help it. She opened her eyes to stare up at his shadowy figure. No one had lit the candle that had been left on the table and she hoped he couldn't see she was awake.

He stood there a moment longer before turning away and leaving the kitchen.

Aschenputtel sat up, staring after him. What had he been thinking as he stood there staring down at her? Had he been remembering his first wife? She didn't know, but guessed she'd better get some sleep. It sounded like Jeanne would be full of orders when she woke and tried to make sure her daughters outshone her. Aschenputtel grinned, wondering what Jeanne would say if she realised who the mysterious lady was. She'd probably lock her up so she couldn't ruin Justine and Yvonne's chances.

Aschenputtel was right. Jeanne threw orders around all day. By the time her family left for the final night of the feast, Aschenputtel was glad to see the last of them. She wandered out the back to the hazel tree, unable to stop herself from asking the little bird to bring her another gown. One to outshine the previous two. She didn't want Lucien to end up with either of her stepsisters. They might be beautiful and have dozens of suitors, but they were as rotten as a maggot filled apple.

The gown was the most exquisite garment she'd ever seen and the slippers were all of gold. As soon as she'd washed and dressed, Aschenputtel again hurried to the castle.

Lucien met her at the ballroom door, taking her hand and staring down at her.

When he remained silent, she dropped into a curtsey. "Your Royal Highness."

"Your beauty leaves me speechless." He took her hand and led her to the gardens. "Where do you disappear to each night?"

"Why I return home, Your Royal Highness."

"I thought we agreed you'd call me Lucien."

She smiled. "I return home, Lucien." She emphasised his name, continuing to smile up at him.

"Tell me about your home."

She had no idea what to say. How could she tell him anything about her life? It would probably disgust him. There was only one thing about her life worth talking about. "I have the dearest friend. A sweet little bird who brings me lovely gifts to brighten my days."

They wandered through the gardens talking and laughing, eventually joining the guests for the meal. Aschenputtel spent the entire night at Lucien's side, dancing with him after the meal.

When a gentleman asked her for a dance, Lucien barely let him get the words out before he spoke. "The lady is my partner, sir." After that, no one else bothered them.

The night grew late and when guests began to leave Aschenputtel looked around. She couldn't see her family. Fearing they'd arrive home before her, she drew away from Lucien. Her gaze focused on him, her heart aching at the thought of never seeing him again. "I must return home."

"Let me escort you there."

Thinking she could slip away from him again, she nodded. This time he remained at her side, leading her out of the ballroom. She couldn't let him see where she lived, couldn't let him learn she was little more than a kitchen wench. When they reached the stairs, she pulled away from him, running down them. In her haste, she lost one of her slippers. There was no time to stop and collect it. Lucien would catch her.

The distance between them grew and she lost him in the streets before turning for home. Seeing her family's carriage pulling up at the front of the house, she went through the garden, leaving her finery at the foot of the hazel tree for the little bird to deal with. She'd barely dressed, covered herself with ashes and curled up on the hearth when she heard her family enter the house. Her stepsisters were complaining bitterly about the woman who'd outshone them all. Aschenputtel smiled, relieved Lucien hadn't been caught by either of them.

Her smile faded as she wondered who he'd end up marrying. He couldn't remain single forever. His father would insist he choose someone or would make the choice for him. Tears filled her eyes and she began to think it would have been better not to have met him. Didn't she have enough heartbreak in her life without having gone seeking more? But she hadn't known. She'd only thought to escape her life for a few days, not fall in love with a prince.

She was the first to rise the next

morning, having been woken by nightmares about Lucien marrying Justine. Unable to sleep further, she went outside and sat at the base of the hazel tree.

The little bird flew out and landed on her shoulder. "What can I do for you?"

She sighed heavily. "Nothing. Just keep me company." Her friend couldn't bring her what she most wanted. She wondered what Lucien was doing. Had he slept as poorly? Or was he even now choosing who was to be his future bride. Sighing once more, she rose to her feet. She should get on with her chores before Jeanne woke and started complaining about how lazy she was.

Surprisingly, Jeanne didn't complain about her at all. She ranted all morning about the mysterious lady. Aschenputtel tried not to smile. She supposed Jeanne actually was complaining about her, even though she didn't realise it. Both her stepsisters joined their mother in her complaints and Aschenputtel was glad her stepsisters decided to visit one of their friends. They were barely gone an hour when they raced into the house, pushing and shoving to be in the lead.

"Mother!" Both of them called out at once.

Justine elbowed her sister. "I'm telling her."

Yvonne shoved at Justine. "You told her last time."

Aschenputtel watched them from the doorway of the parlour she'd been about to enter.

Jeanne rose from her seat, setting aside her needlework. "Enough.

Show some decorum. What is so important you should almost come to blows over it?"

"The prince is coming," Justine said at the same time as Yvone said, "Prince Lucien has said he'll marry whoever fits the slipper."

"Quiet." Jeanne turned to Justine. "Start from the beginning and tell me exactly what is going on."

Aschenputtel clung to the doorframe, thinking about the slipper she'd left behind. There were probably a number of women who'd fit the slipper. She couldn't be the only woman with small feet.

"The mysterious lady left behind one of her slippers. King Percevel is livid his son won't choose a bride. It's all over the town that they argued this morning and Prince Lucien held up the slipper and said he'd only marry the woman who can fit the slipper she left behind. He's been travelling from house to house and the ladies have been trying to squeeze their feet into it," Justine said.

"Hurry," Jeanne waved them from the room. "You must prepare yourselves for your bridegroom. Put on your finest gowns."

Aschenputtel stepped out of the doorway, not wanting to be caught listening in on them.

"What if we don't fit it?" Yvonne asked.

"We'll make it fit." Jeanne sailed from the room, her daughters following in her wake.

Aschenputtel stared after them, thinking about her nightmare. Surely he wouldn't marry one of her stepsisters. She tried to think of something she could do, but there was nothing.

Claude came into the hallway. "What's all the fuss about?"

Aschenputtel looked around, but there was no one else to answer him. "Lu… Prince Lucien is searching for his bride." She'd nearly called him by his first name.

"He's coming here? To marry one of my daughters?"

Aschenputtel shrugged.

"I'd better go and see if they need anything."

She breathed in sharply as he walked away, unshed tears making her throat ache. Running from the house, she went to the hazel tree, throwing herself on the ground. "Don't let him marry them. Please don't let him marry them."

The bird flew out to land on her

shoulder. "Their feet will not fit your slipper."

She dashed away her tears. "They won't?"

"No. Your feet are far more dainty than theirs."

Relief rushed through her. "Thank you." She put up her hand so the bird could hop onto it. "Thank you, my dearest friend." She dropped a kiss onto his head and lifted her hand so he could fly back to the tree. Taking a calming breath, she wiped the last of the tears from her face and returned to the kitchen.

When Lucien arrived and was shown to the parlour, Aschenputtel crept close to catch a glimpse of him. She wanted to run into the room and beg him to let her try on the slipper too. A footman stood beside him, holding the slipper. Lucien waved the footman forward.

Jeanne stepped between the footman and Justine. "Surely you don't expect my daughter to try the slipper on in front of two gentleman. How undignified." She took the slipper from the footman. "We will be back in a minute."

Aschenputtel fled to the kitchen, slipping into a shadowy corner when the three of them entered the room.

"How will I ever fit my foot into the slipper?" Justine demanded. "It looks like it belongs to a child."

"Sit down. We'll make it fit." Jeanne gestured to one of the chairs at the kitchen table.

Aschenputtel watched as Jeanne tried to force Justine's foot into the slipper. Relief washed over her when they failed.

"My big toe keeps getting in the way," Justine complained.

Jeanne grabbed a knife. "Then we'll get rid of it."

Justine jumped to her feet. "No. How can you say something like that?"

"Let me try," Yvonne said.

"Do you want to marry a prince?" Jeanne demanded.

Justine nodded.

"When you eventually become the queen you won't care about toes. Sit down and let me cut off your big toe. And don't you dare make a sound."

Aschenputtel couldn't believe Justine sat down and let her mother cut off her toe. She watched as her stepsister paled, but didn't make a sound. Instead she clutched the back of the chair, her knuckles white from her grip. Once the toe was gone, the slipper slid on easily.

Jeanne wiped the blood from the slipper and rose to her feet. "Now let's go and show your bridegroom."

Aschenputtel couldn't bring herself to follow them. She sunk to the floor where she stood, drawing her legs up and wrapping her arms around them. Her nightmare was about to come true. Jeanne had made the slipper fit Justine. She had no idea how long she sat there, but eventually she rose to check in the parlour. Jeanne and Yvonne were sitting there congratulating themselves, Claude beaming proudly. Aschenputtel went to the front door and peeked outside. She was surprised to see Lucien riding back towards the house, Justine seated sideways before him, an angry expression on her face. The footman rode beside them. What had happened? Aschenputtel didn't know, but she couldn't risk being caught spying at the door. She hurried to the kitchen, waiting until Lucien was ushered inside before she returned to peeking around the edge of the parlour door.

Lucien pointed towards Justine. "You tried to trick me by cutting off her toe."

Jeanne shook her head. "Certainly not, Your Royal Highness."

"Look at her foot. If a little bird hadn't called out to me as I rode away telling me to look at the foot of my false bride I would have taken her home."

Jeanne checked Justine's foot. "You deceitful girl. How dare you?"

"But–"

Justine's words were cut off by a

slap from her mother. "Go to your room." Jeanne turned to Lucien. "I'm terribly sorry, Your Royal Highness. I'll keep a better eye on my younger daughter." At Lucien's nod, she took the slipper from the footman.

Aschenputtel, who'd momentarily stepped out of the way to let Justine through, hurried to the kitchen and hid in the shadowy corner again. She watched as Jeanne seated Yvonne at the table and tried to force the slipper on her.

"The slipper's too small." Yvonne glared at her heel, which wouldn't fit in.

"We'll make it fit." Jeanne took the knife she'd used on her eldest daughter. "I'll cut off your heel."

Yvonne drew up her foot. "It didn't work for Justine."

"The foolish girl must have given

herself away. Whoever heard of a bird talking?"

"He'll see the blood."

"Not if we bind it. Now quit stalling and give me your foot. Don't you want to be a queen one day?"

Yvonne lowered her foot to the floor. "Of course I do."

Aschenputtel watched as her stepsister gasped, her eyes filling with tears. She felt a moment of sympathy for Yvonne, but forced it away with memories of all the nasty things her stepsister had done to her.

"It's so painful," Yvonne wailed.

"Oh hush. Do you want them to hear you?" Finished, Jeanne bound the foot and pushed it in the slipper. "There, all done. Now, don't say a word."

Yvonne whimpered, wiping at the tears with the back of one hand. She rose to her feet and walked slowly from the kitchen. Jeanne followed her.

Aschenputtel stepped away from the corner, trying to decide if she should follow. Would Lucien check that the slipper fit properly this time? Crossing the room, she paused in the doorway, listening. Had they already left? She silently made her way to the parlour and peeked around the doorway. Her parents were in there, smiling at each other, talking about how life would change when Yvonne married the prince. Aschenputtel moved away, not wanting to listen to another word. Would her little bird warn Lucien again? She was afraid he wouldn't. But even if the bird warned him, that didn't mean she'd have the chance to try on the slipper.

What was she thinking? She was

dressed in rags, covered in ash and looked nothing like the lady Lucien searched for. She'd nearly given up when she heard them returning, Yvonne wailing loudly. She slipped away so no one would see her, watching from the kitchen doorway as Yvonne led Lucien into the parlour. She hurried forward in time to hear Lucien speak.

"Once again a little bird told me I hadn't found my true bride and you had tried to deceive me."

Aschenputtel saw that this time it was Lucien who held the slipper and he didn't look happy. She was relieved her friend had saved him from the clutches of her stepsisters.

Jeanne clasped her hands together. "Your Royal Highness, I cannot imagine what my foolish girls were thinking." She turned to Yvonne. "Go to your room and stay there."

Yvonne hobbled from the room, still wailing. Aschenputtel, who'd stepped out of the way, peered back into the room.

"Have you no other daughters?" Lucien asked.

Claude shook his head. "No, there's only a dirty little kitchen wench, the daughter of my first wife."

His words hurt and she nearly burst into the room to tell him she was his daughter too. Jeanne's words stopped her.

"There's no point asking her to present herself. She's so dirty she'd be ashamed to show her face to you, Your Royal Highness."

Aschenputtel looked down at herself as she listened to Lucien tell her parents to fetch her. Jeanne was right. How could she face Lucien looking like this? She never wanted to see that same look of disgust on his face that she regularly saw on Jeanne's. She ran to the kitchen, planning to retreat to the hazel tree. She stopped in the doorway, unable to bring herself to take another step away from Lucien. Someone was sure to fit the slipper. Lucien would keep looking until he found someone. She couldn't bear to think of Lucien married to anyone else. Turning around, she fetched water and washed her hands and face. It wasn't much of an improvement, but it was all she had time for. She strode back to the parlour, hoping they hadn't left.

Jeanne was the first to notice her. "What are you doing here?"

Ignoring Jeanne, Aschenputtel crossed the room to stand in front of Lucien, who looked surprised. She dropped into a curtsy, wondering if it was because he recognise her or if he was amazed a dirty kitchen wench had the audacity to present herself to him. When she rose, she reached for the slipper, removing her own clumsy boot before sliding her foot into it. She met Lucien's gaze, relieved to see surprise had been replaced by a smile. "Your Royal Highness, I believe the slipper fits."

Lucien chuckled. "How many times must I ask you to call me Lucien?"

"No!" Jeanne's roar prevented any reply Aschenputtel might have made.

Lucien turned to Jeanne. "This one is the right bride." Turning to Aschenputtel, he held out his hand.

She willingly took it and was surprised when he raised her hand to his lips. Not to mention relieved she'd taken the time to wash it.

He met her gaze over her hand, lowering it as he took a step closer. "Shall we go home?"

She nodded, walking beside him to the front of the house where his horse waited. He swung up into the saddle and held his hand out so he could set her before him. She couldn't bring herself to take it, afraid her dirty clothes would ruin his immaculate outfit.

"Don't you wish to become my bride?" Concern crossed his face. "After all those hours we spent together talking and dancing I had thought…" His voice trailed off.

Seeing some of her own fears reflected back at her in his expression helped hers disappear. She took his hand and let him help her onto the horse so she could sit sideways in front of him. Turning her face, she met his gaze. "I couldn't think of anything I'd rather do." She returned Lucien's smile, facing forward when the horse began to walk away from the house.

The sound of wings drew their attention and Lucien chuckled when the little bird landed on her shoulder. "I had a feeling it was your friend when he spoke to me earlier."

Aschenputtel was glad the little bird was coming with her. She smiled. She'd underestimated her friend that morning when he'd asked her what he could do for her. It looked like he'd helped her after all. "Yes, he's one of my dearest friends and I'm grateful he came into my life." She thought back to the moment she'd asked her father for the twig, trying to remind him of her mother. Instead it had brought her something far more precious than just the little bird. Her gaze met Lucien's and held it. "Without him I would never have met you."

"Then he's one of my dearest friends too."

The Light Princess

In a quest to find a bride, Prince Ruairidh stumbles upon The Light Princess, a completely inappropriate bride with an unbreakable spell upon her. He hears rumours that it was her aunt, Princess Makemnoit, who put the spell on her, but no one knows for certain. The Light Princess would make no one a suitable bride, least of all a prince. But when she's in the lake there's something about her that intrigues Prince Ruairidh and he can't help wanting to spend more time with her.

*

People have been telling stories since the beginning of time. Fairytales, folklore, myths and legends are among some of the stories that have been told over and over through the centuries. The basic story remains the same, but each storyteller adds their own style, sometimes adding something unique to the tale.

*

This story was written by an Australian author using Australian spelling.

Name Pronunciation

Like many names there is more than one way to pronounce the following ones. These are the pronunciations used in this story.

Moire (moy-rah)

Ruairidh (roo-ah-ree)

Makemnoit (may-kem-noy-t)

Ailig (al-ic)

Chapter One
Princess Makemnoit

Princess Makemnoit paced back and forth in her kitchen, fuming at yet another insult. First her father, the king, left her nothing in his will, leaving it all to her brother. Her younger brother. Now her brother, the current king, didn't bother to send her an invite to the christening of his long awaited daughter. How dare they forget her? She'd show all of them that she wasn't to be forgotten.

She'd make her brother regret the day he forgot he ever had a sister.

Stopping in front of an old chest, she flung open the lid to take several ingredients from it. She threw them into the pot, hanging over the fire, as it started to bubble. The liquid in the pot darkened, large bubbles popping on the surface. When it cleared, Princess Makemnoit grabbed a vial and spooned some of the liquid into it. This would be the last time anyone would forget her. She'd make sure of it.

Setting the vial on the window ledge, ready to take with her when she left for the palace in the morning, Princess Makemnoit sat in her rocking chair by the fire. Staring into the flames, she chuckled. The morning couldn't come soon enough. Her black cat jumped onto her lap, turning several times before he curled up, tucking his tail close to his body.

Princess Makemnoit stroked the cat who began to purr. "You never forget me, do you?" The cat opened an eye and momentarily peered up at her before he closed it again. She slowly rocked the chair as she thought of her plan. The most cunning of plans. No one would have a clue how to undo what she was about to do. And no one would ever dare forget her again.

The next morning, Princess Makemnoit dressed in her best garment. A worn silk dress, the once dark green fabric now faded, the cuffs of the sleeves frayed. Once, a long time ago, she'd had fine clothes, new ones every year. That was until she was left out of the will. She picked up the vial, staring at the clear liquid. Her brother was long past overdue for this punishment. He'd never once argued against the will, accepting everything for himself, leaving her with nothing. She'd been forced to leave the castle and move into a cottage, a long way from town, in the forest bordering the lake that the castle overlooked. She pocketed the vial before setting out to the palace, the long walk making her feet ache in her worn shoes. Upon reaching the gates, she was ushered inside by one of the guards and taken straight to the king and queen.

The king came forward, his hands held out to take hers, a smile on his face. "Sister, so good that you could join us."

Princess Makemnoit took his hands, pasting a smile on her own face. How dare he act like he'd invited her? Lying swine! "I wouldn't have missed this momentous occasion for anything." She directed her smile towards the queen. "Especially since we had begun to despair you would ever have a child, my dearest sister."

The queen returned the smile, cradling her baby, who was already dressed in her lacy finery. The nurse hovered at her shoulder, waiting to take the young princess.

"Yes, yes." The king's smile faltered. "We should leave for the church. It wouldn't do to be late."

Princess Makemnoit's own smile widened. "No, of course not. It would be inconsiderate after all the waiting the people have already done." She joined the royal procession, making certain she was near the font when they arrived at the church. She patiently waited until the last moment, making sure no one was watching, and poured the contents of the vial into the water. She spun three times on the spot, muttering the words of the spell under her breath.

The priest froze, staring at her in astonishment, and a murmur went through the crowd.

"Are you well, sister?" the king asked.

Princess Makemnoit continued to smile. "Of course I am. This is such a momentous occasion I can barely contain my joy for you." Her smile widened as her brother gestured towards the priest and the child was baptised.

She carefully watched the infant laugh as the water trickled off her head, and saw the nurse's startled expression when the child was handed back to her. It looked like the spell was working. News of the princess' problem was sure to be all around the countryside within days.

But it wasn't. Princess Makemnoit waited to hear the smallest of rumours, but there were none. She fumed and waited. When several months passed, she began to think that her spell might have failed. She checked all the ingredients she had used, finding them still usable. What could have gone wrong? She'd have to figure out something else to do instead. But that had been her best spell, the most powerful one she knew. Obviously she needed to learn more spells. Powerful ones that no one could undo. Several days later, her brother came knocking on her door.

"Why, brother, what a pleasant

surprise. Come in." Princess Makemnoit stepped out of the doorway so he could enter. Why was he here? Hope arrowed through her and she smiled. "You should have sent word you were coming. I have no refreshments prepared."

"This isn't a social call, sister. I cannot understand what I have done wrong, but heartily apologise for any offence I might have unwittingly offered you."

Princess Makemnoit replaced her smile with an expression of concern, not wanting to admit to anything yet. "Why whatever do you mean?"

"My daughter. You have cast a spell on her. I know it must have been you. There is no one else who could have done this."

She tried very hard to look shocked and keep the smile from returning to her face. "How could you even think that of me? Why, I'd never cause any harm to my darling niece. Whatever is the matter with her?"

"She has no gravity. A gold coin weighs more than the princess. And she laughs. At everything. At the most inappropriate times. We have almost lost her several times. A puff of wind can carry her away. Like a dandelion seed on the breeze, drifting along until it comes to rest on the ground. We found her under a rose bush." His voice grew louder. "A rose bush!" He took a deep breath, visibly trying to calm himself, lowering his voice. "Please, you must take the spell off my daughter."

"I would love to be able to help you, but I have no idea what you're talking about."

"Please."

Princess Makemnoit shook her head, continuing to deny the accusations even when the king became demanding and finally began to shout. When he left she danced around the room, her steps leading her into the kitchen where she scooped up her cat.

"They'll never find a cure and their lives will be miserable with their light headed child. Nor will they ever find someone to marry her. For who would take seriously one who takes nothing seriously?" And most important of all, the princess would never learn to love anyone. Princess Makemnoit laughed as she spun around the kitchen, holding her cat close. "That will teach them not to forget me. They might not know for certain it was me, but they suspect and that will keep them cautious."

Again she laughed. Never again would she be forgotten. They'd always remember her now.

Chapter Two
Prince Ruairidh

Prince Ruairidh mounted his horse trying to make his smile contain at least some of the friendliness of the smiles directed at him. But he couldn't match the cheerful grins of the Princess and her parents who waved enthusiastically to him. Once he was astride his horse, he sent one more smile in their direction, gave them a halfhearted wave and rode towards the gates, his entourage following him. Why couldn't he have been born a merchant's son? He'd met several merchants' daughters that had more than their looks to recommend them.

As he travelled along the well-kept road, he thought about all the princesses he'd met. A sea of faces filled his mind. He'd thought that by visiting other countries he'd finally meet a princess he could tolerate for more than a couple of hours. So far he'd failed. He couldn't travel forever. Eventually he'd have to return home and marry one of the princesses his parents had suggested. He dreaded to think how terrible his life would become.

"Where to now, Your Royal Highness?" one of his courtiers asked.

Ruairidh looked around. The road led straight ahead, uneventful and boring. Like the princess he'd left behind. To his left a forest pressed up against the road, open meadows out to his right. It only took a moment to make up his mind. "This way." He turned his horse towards the forest, making his own path.

"Your Royal Highness, do you think this is wise?" the courtier asked.

Ruairidh grinned, almost laughing at the shocked tone in his courtier's voice. "No, but it's a vast improvement over the path we were on." He urged his horse forward, trotting ahead of his entourage. Through the trees he spotted a stag and automatically gave chase. Behind him he heard his entourage do the same, the sound of hoof beats eventually fading behind him. By the time he had lost the stag, Ruairidh realised he'd also lost his entourage. Not even a guard was in sight. He was alone for the first time in his entire life and it actually felt good.

Ruairidh chuckled as he thought of his entourage frantically searching for him. He wouldn't have to worry about trying to find them. Eventually they'd find him. He continued through the forest, the shadows lengthening as the day drew to a close. Ahead of him he saw a light and rode towards it, finding a cottage nestled amongst the trees. Dismounting, he knocked on the door.

A man opened the door, his brown hair and beard sprinkled with grey, his shoulders broad and his brown eyes checking the prince over before peering behind him. "Are you lost, my lord?"

Ruairidh nodded. "You could say that." He held out his hand, deciding it would be best not to mention he was a prince. You could never be too careful. "I'm Ruairidh and I'm afraid I lost my companions in the forest. I dare say they'll wander out eventually, but I'm in need of a place to stay for the night."

The man took his hand. "Ailig." He stepped back. "I was sitting down to eat. It isn't much, but you're welcome to share it, my lord."

Ruairidh came in, closing the door behind him. "Please, call me Ruairidh." He sat in the seat Ailig indicated, at a small wooden table. A glance around showed the cottage consisted of a single, small room, a narrow bed along the far wall and a trunk beside it. The table and two chairs were the only other furniture if you didn't count the small shelf high on the wall beside the fire.

Ailig took a bowl from the shelf and ladled stew from the pot hanging over the fire. "I don't get many visitors out this way. Most stick to the road." He collected a spoon off the shelf and put it and the bowl in front of Ruairidh, sitting in the other seat where there was already a bowl. "How did you come to leave the road?"

"I was chasing a stag. With antlers this wide." He stretched his arms out. "I lost him though. And my companions too."

Ailig nodded. "Easily done."

"So where am I? And how far away is the nearest town?" He had a mouthful of the stew. "This is good." He indicated the bowl with his spoon.

"Lagobel. The closest town is about

half a day away. You'll reach the castle before you reach it."

"The castle?"

"They don't get many visitors there. Even with a princess of marriageable age. Seventeen and not a single suitor. I guess none of them want to be laughed at, or wonder if their children will have her affliction."

Ruairidh's food lay forgotten in his bowl. "Affliction?"

Ailig nodded again. "The poor lass hasn't a bit of gravity. Lighter than a cloud on a summer day. Why they even had to get the chimney sweep to fetch her out of the chimney once. A great gust of air blew her up there and they were afraid she'd be blown clear across the country. The king now makes twenty noblemen, on horseback, go with her wherever she goes and each ties a silken cord to her and never lets it go."

Ruairidh stared across the table. "Surely not." The man must think him simple to swallow a tale like that.

"Only take yourself on over to the castle come morning and see for yourself. Prettiest lass in the land, but her head is as light as the rest of her. And I'm not talking about how light in colour her hair is. Although it is fair. No, not a serious thought has ever entered her head and she laughs at everything, including a person's misfortunes."

"Was she born like that?"

"No. She was like any other child until her christening. There's rumours. There always is about things like this. But me, I say the king's sister is the one who did it. Ugly old hag that she is. Never cross that one. She's a witch." Ailig nodded his head emphatically.

"Surely there must be a way to break the spell. Every spell has some way of being broken."

Ailig shrugged. "Maybe, but if there is, not a single person has figured it out in all these years. And the king has certainly tried. He's had all sorts of people working on the problem and not a single one of them could find a cure." He shook his head. "No. The lass will be like that for the rest of her life. Empty headed and lacking gravity." He pointed to Ruairidh's bowl. "You better eat up, my lord. Your food will be getting cold."

Ruairidh looked down at his bowl, having forgotten it was there. As he finished his meal he couldn't help thinking about the princess. It might be worth having a look, just to make sure Ailig wasn't telling him a tale. He certainly couldn't marry a princess who found even the misfortunes of others amusing, but at least she should be a temporary diversion from his task of needing to find himself a wife.

"What is her name?"

"Who?" Ailig asked.

"The princess. What is her name?"

"Princess Moire, but most around here call her The Light Princess." Ailig rose to his feet, gathering up the two empty bowls. "I've only one bed, but you can have it and I'll make myself a place by the fire."

While Ailig tidied up, Ruairidh tried to convince him it wasn't necessary to give up his bed. Eventually he gave in and thanked the man, retiring for the night. He lay awake for ages, wondering what type of person could laugh at the misfortunes of others. Not the sort who would make a good ruler of any country. He hoped the king and queen had more than the one child or their country would be in trouble when neither of them were no longer around to run it.

After a breakfast of porridge the next morning, Ruairidh went hunting with Ailig, wanting to help out in exchange for the food and warm bed. It wasn't until afternoon that he swung up onto his horse and set out for the castle. As the sun was setting, he saw a moor through the thinning trees, a lake surrounded by woodland in the distance with a castle overlooking it. Reaching the woodland, he dismounted and tied up his weary horse, continuing on foot along a narrow path that led him to the side of the lake. Light from the sinking sun coloured the water. He reached the edge of the lake as the last of the light faded and sounds reached him across the water.

Splashing and what might be screaming or shrieking. The type of sounds that usually meant someone was in trouble. He kicked off his boots, removed his shirt and unbuckled his sword. Leaving his gear on the ground, he strode into the lake, swimming towards the sound once the water was deep enough. He found a woman shrieking as she splashed about in the water. Fearing she was drowning, he towed her to shore, trying to subdue her frantic movements.

Somehow he reached a part of the shore that was different to where he'd entered and the bank was about a foot above him. Treading water, he hoisted the woman up, planning to put her on the bank, but she continued to rise, a white robed figure slowly going higher. For a moment he thought that maybe he'd mistaken a swan for a woman.

"How dare you! What did you think you were doing?" the woman shrieked.

"Rescuing you." Ruairidh heaved himself out of the water and stood dripping on the shore, watching the shadowy figure of the woman rise higher into the sky.

"I didn't need rescuing."

Ruairidh hurried forward, trying to see the woman clearer. She was caught in the branches of a pine tree, clasping a pinecone in one hand, holding onto a branch with the other. "You sounded like you did."

"What business had you to pull me down out of the water, and throw me to the bottom of the air?"

Ruairidh stared at her as she inched her way down the tree, trying to make sense of her words. "I'm sorry."

The woman reached the ground, grabbing hold of his arm to keep herself there. "I don't believe you have any brains and that is a worse loss than gravity. Stupid man." She stamped her foot, only her hold on his arm keeping her there.

Moonlight now shone down on them and Ruairidh was able to see the woman clearer. The blond, beautiful young woman had to be Princess Moire, or The Light Princess as her people called her. What a pity she was bewitched. She had to be the most fascinating princess he'd ever met.

"Well? Have you lost the power of speech as well as your mind?"

"Maybe I have been made speechless by your beauty." He grinned, expecting her to reply with one of the frivolous comments princesses normally used.

"Put me up directly."

Her words surprised him. "Put you up where?"

"In the water, stupid!"

He chuckled. No one had ever called him that before. At least not to his face. "Come, then." He held onto her hand and walked further around the lake, hoping to find a shallow area to enter. Her wet dress caught around her legs and he started to offer to carry her, but decided against it when he saw her expression. Obviously it was only the misfortunes of others that she laughed at, not her own.

The further they travelled around the lake, the longer the drop into the water became until it was at least twenty-five feet down. Ruairidh stared at the moonlit dappled water below them. "How am I to put you in?"

"That is your business," she snapped. "You took me out, you put me in."

He could think of only one method. "Very well." He caught her up in his arms and leapt over the edge.

The princess gave a shriek of laughter before the water closed over them. When they surfaced she was gasping for breath, but grinning.

Ruairidh grinned back at her. "How do you like falling in?"

"Is that what you call falling in?"

He nodded. "Yes, I should think it

a very tolerable example of it." She continued to remain in the circle of his arms as he tread water.

"It seemed to me like going up."

He laughed. "My feeling was certainly one of elevation." He continued to hold her, not wanting to let go.

Moire looked confused for a moment. "How do you like falling in?"

He stared at her for a moment. "Rather more than I had expected to." Maybe Ailig had been wrong. Surely the young woman in his arms wouldn't laugh at the misfortune of others. And she certainly wasn't as light of mind as she was of weight, although in the water she seemed to have no problem with gravity. "It was beyond everything for I have fallen in with the only perfect creature I ever saw."

"Enough of that nonsense," Moire said sternly.

He made a mental note that unlike other princesses she didn't like flattery. "Don't you like falling in, then?"

"It's the most delightful fun I've had in my entire life. I have never fallen before. I wish I could learn. To think I'm the only person in the kingdom that can't fall!"

At the sad expression that crossed her face, Ruairidh hurriedly said, "I'll fall into the lake with you again another day. Every day if you wish." He wanted to spend more time with her, wanted to get to know her. She fascinated him more than anyone ever had.

"Thank you, but I don't know.

Perhaps it wouldn't be proper. But I don't care." She laughed. "It was the most amazing feeling." She drew away from him. "Let's swim together."

Not wanting his time with the princess to end too soon, Ruairidh agreed and they swam and dived into the water, eventually floating on the surface of the lake, speaking until late into the night. Their evening was eventually interrupted by shouts from the shore, lights bobbing along as people called for the princess.

Moire sat up, treading water. "I must go home, although I don't really want to. I've had a delightful evening. I wish it would never end."

"So do I."

"This is so stupid. They're ruining my fun. I've a mind to play a trick on all of them. Why couldn't they leave me alone? They won't trust me in the lake for a single night! You see where that green light is burning? That's the window of my room. Now if you would just swim there with me very quietly, and when we are under the balcony, give me what you call a push up. I'll be able to catch hold of the balcony and get in at the window. Then they can look for me till tomorrow morning for all I care."

Ruairidh reluctantly agreed, wishing she didn't have to return home at all. When they reached the place beneath her balcony, he lifted her out of the water and watched as she grabbed hold of the balcony. "Will you be in the lake tomorrow?"

"To be sure I will. I don't think so. Perhaps."

He frowned, trying to make sense of her words. "Don't tell anyone about me." He wanted to get to know her without all her entourage watching over them. What had Ailig said? Twenty noblemen. Far more people than a princess usually had following her around.

"Never fear. It was too good fun to spoil by telling anyone."

He watched her rise in the air, laughter trailing in her wake, until she disappeared inside. In the water she had seemed so normal that he'd completely forgotten she was without gravity. He stared at her window a moment longer before he swam across the lake, looking for the place where he'd left his gear. Luckily those looking for the princess hadn't made it that far and he pulled on his boots before he searched for somewhere to spend the rest of the night. It was too far to travel back to Ailig's cottage.

He soon found a spot from where he could see the green light in the princess's room. It was a shallow cave in the rocks and a scattering of leaves, blown in there from the trees that edged the lake, formed a bed for him to sleep on. He lay down, too tired for hunger to keep him awake, and dreamt that he was swimming with the princess.

As soon as the sun rose the following morning, Ruairidh returned to Ailig's cottage rather than risk running into his entourage in the town. He left his horse with Ailig, giving the man some coins in exchange for supplies and asking him numerous questions about Moire before he returned to the lake and his cave. It was late afternoon and the lake was filled with little boats, canopies of all the colours of the rainbow and a great many flags and streamers.

He saw the king and queen in one of the boats, lords and ladies filling the others. In the water was the princess. Ruairidh watched Moire, wishing he could join her. It wasn't until the sun was setting that the boats returned to the shore and Moire was alone in the water, having won the argument with her parents to stay longer.

Ruairidh walked around the lake to an area that rose up above the water and sat on a rock, singing a popular song about a beautiful lady and a lake. Moire didn't start to swim towards him, until he'd nearly reached the end of the song. When she reached the edge of the lake, she tread water, looking up at him.

He stopped singing to smile down

at her. "Would you like a fall, princess?"

"Yes, if you please, prince."

"How do you know I'm a prince?"

"You sound like one, besides, you gave me no other name to call you by."

Ruairidh laughed. In all their conversations the night before they hadn't once exchanged names. He removed his shirt and belt, tying the two together and lowered them over the edge. "Come up then, princess." He pulled her up once she grabbed the end, her weight becoming nothing as soon as she was out of the water.

Moire clung to him when she was on the land. "I'm ready to fall in."

"I was thinking we might go a little further along the shore. It's a much bigger jump." When she nodded, he kicked off his boots, wrapped his arms around her and leaving his gear on the ground, carried her along the shore. He stood on the edge, his gaze meeting hers in the moonlight. "I'm Ruairidh." Then he jumped.

They surfaced together, Moire's laugh ringing out in the night. "That was better than the last one, Ruairidh. I want to fall in again."

"Tomorrow night."

She nodded. "Then if you won't help me fall in again, let's swim."

Like the night before they swam and dived, eventually floating on the lake, speaking until it was late. Night after night Ruairidh met Moire in the lake, starting the night out by jumping in with her. Weeks passed and he didn't even give his entourage a thought, except for the couple of occasions when he returned to Ailig's cottage for supplies and reminded the man not to tell anyone he'd seen him.

The few moments each evening that Moire was on the shore with him, Ruairidh found her to be a completely different person. He began to think about asking her to marry him and wondered how they could rule a country from the lake. It seemed that the lake let Moire be herself. Once out of it, she became empty headed and strange, most of her comments and questions not making any sense.

But even in the lake, when Ruairidh mentioned love, Moire seemed confused as if she didn't know what he spoke about. He hoped that as more time passed she'd finally learn and then he could ask her to marry him. He couldn't imagine a life without her.

Chapter Three
Princess Makemnoit

Princess Makemnoit trudged along the shore, determined to see for herself if the rumours were true. It was late afternoon and she could clearly see Princess Moire diving about in the water, her laughter reaching the shore. And it wasn't the odd, emotionless laugh she gave when she was on land. No, this laugh was filled with pleasure and joy. Princess Makemnoit's hands curled into fists. There was the king and queen in one of the boats on the lake, looking just as happy as their daughter. She wasn't having it. They were being punished. They shouldn't be happy. Every last one of them should be miserable. Completely and utterly miserable.

With one more glare at the lake, Princess Makemnoit turned away and strode back to her cottage. The situation had to be dealt with. And she knew exactly what needed to be done.

"The king and the people shall die of thirst. Their brains shall boil and frizzle in their skulls and I will have my revenge." They would all pay this time. Every one of them. From the babies not yet born to the old people about to die and all in between. They were all guilty and all would pay.

Going to an old chest in her room,

she unlocked it. Pulling out what looked like a piece of dried seaweed, she took it to the kitchen where she threw it into a large pot of water. Next she tossed in some powder and stirred it with her bare arm, muttering words over it. Then she set the pot aside. For a moment she stared at it, watching the seaweed like item swirl around in the liquid, slowly changing shape.

Turning away, she gathered a bunch of a hundred rusty keys that clattered in her shaking hands, and sat down to oil them. She could barely contain her excitement. Never had she expected to be using this spell she'd discovered. And never had she ever expected to use the special cavern that had been made by the witch who'd owned this cottage long before she had. The witch who'd shown her so many amazing things during her childhood and taught her the first spell she'd learned.

She'd been heartbroken the day the witch had died and had often visited her cottage to read through the spell books and tend the herb garden. The witch had been the only one who'd ever cared for her. She had also been ostracised by the town. They'd pay for that too. They had so many sins to atone for. Princess Makemnoit chuckled. Oh how they would pay. And they'd keep on paying.

Before she'd finished oiling the keys, a huge grey snake emerged from the pot. It slithered across the floor to her and raised itself up to rest around her shoulders. She dropped a kiss on its head, smiling in anticipation.

"My darling White Snake of

Darkness, I have a little job for you." She continued to oil the keys as the snake hissed in her ear, its forked tongue flickering out. "Soon, very soon." She couldn't wait. They'd learn. She'd make certain of it this time. None of them would be able to undo this. None would be willing.

Once the keys were oiled, she grabbed a basket and a lit lantern and went down to her cellar, unlocking the door at the far end of the room, her black cat at her heels. Locking it behind her, she turned to face a dark, narrow passage, another door ahead of her. She continued along the downward sloping passage, unlocking and locking doors as she went, the snake coiled around her shoulders, its tail dragging behind her.

Eventually she reached the final

door and entered a vast cave, the roof of which was supported by huge natural pillars of rock. She untwined the snake from her body, and held it above her. The creature stretched towards the roof of the cavern, moving its head backwards and forwards, as if looking for something, its tail resting on the ground.

Letting go of the snake, Princess Makemnoit headed for the outer edge of the cavern. She began to walk round and round the cavern, coming nearer to the centre with every circuit. The head of the snake described the same path over the roof that she did on the floor. Round and round the cavern they went, until the snake darted forward and clung to the roof with its mouth.

"That's it my darling White Snake of Darkness. Drain the lake until it's dry," Princess Makemnoit cried out. "Drain every last drop. Then the springs and streams that feed it can drain into here on their own."

She watched the snake for several minutes then sat down on a large stone, the black cat still at her side, and took her knitting from her basket. For seven days and seven nights they remained in the cavern, the witch feeding herself and the cat from the food in her basket. Then the bloated snake dropped from the cavern roof, shrivelling up until once again it looked like a piece of dried seaweed. Princess Makemnoit returned her knitting to her basket, collected the shrivelled snake and crossed to the centre of the cavern to peer up at the roof.

Above her a single drop of water hung for a moment before falling to the cavern floor. Another drop soon joined it. With a smile, Princess Makemnoit gathered her things. The cat followed at her heel as she returned through the hundred doors, locking each one behind her as she hurried along. She was halfway along before she started to hear the sound of rushing water behind her. The drip had become a gush. Still smiling, she locked her cellar door, heading to her kitchen to drop exhausted into her rocking chair.

Tomorrow she'd see what the lake looked like. For now she needed to rest. Her cat jumped up on her lap and began to purr when she patted him. "They'll learn. All of them." The cat purred louder as if he agreed.

Princess Makemnoit drifted off to sleep in front of the fire, woken by the morning light coming in the kitchen window. She shooed the cat from her lap and after breakfast, walked to the lake to check the level of the water. It wasn't enough. The streams that fed the lake were keeping it from sinking too quickly. She had to stop them. Returning home, she took some of the water in which she'd revived the snake, put it in a bottle, and set out accompanied by her cat. By the early hours of the morning she'd walked around the lake, muttering the words of her spell as she crossed every stream, casting some water from her bottle into it. Half the night she'd had to endure the laughter of Princess Moire and that of some unknown man as they played in the lake. She gritted her teeth, relieved when the princess returned to her room and the man left. Soon, very soon they'd learn not to forget her. This time she'd make it impossible for them to forget her.

When Princess Makemnoit finished her circuit of the lake she said the final words of the spell and flung a handful of water towards the setting moon. She felt all the springs in the country cease to bubble, and cackling, headed for home. By nightfall the streams would stop running and the lake would drop even faster. Princess Moire would have nowhere to swim and have to spend her every moment empty headed and lacking in gravity. One day she might tell them it was her, but for now she would continue to let them wonder. It was more fun that way. Besides, keeping them uncertain made them wary of her. And that was good.

Chapter Four
Prince Ruairidh

Holding Moire in his arms, Ruairidh jumped into the lake, grinning when he surfaced. His grin faded when Moire didn't laugh like she usually did. "Moire? Didn't you like falling in?"

"Does the lake seem lower than usual?" Without waiting for his answer, she swam for shore, reaching one of the low banks.

Ruairidh followed her, stepping out onto the shore while she stayed in the water. "I'm not certain, but I think it could be. I'm sure it'll rise again once your rainy season begins."

Moire picked up a rock in each hand and stepped onto the shore, shaking her head. "It never changes. Years and years and it never changes." She walked back into the lake, dropping the rocks and swimming towards the castle.

"Moire?" Ruairidh called out to her, but she kept swimming. By the time he realised she was returning home, she was too far ahead for him to catch up with her. Instead he returned to his cave and slept fitfully as he waited for morning.

He rose with the sun and watched for Moire. It wasn't a long wait. She came with twenty noblemen on horseback, each holding a silken cord that was tied to various parts of her body. She walked along the lake only a short way before she turned and ran back towards the castle. A gust of wind caught her and she floated into the sky, only the silken cords keeping her from blowing away.

That night she didn't come and Ruairidh swam through the lake and tread water beneath her balcony. He sang the song he'd sung the first time he'd tried to catch her attention. Moire didn't appear at her window. Days passed and Ruairidh returned to Ailig's cottage to see what he knew. The lake had now shrunk noticeably and Ruairidh hoped the rainy season would arrive soon. He didn't want to spend months without Moire. The days were colourless without her.

Ailig was out behind his cottage, chopping firewood. He paused in the task when he saw Ruairidh, leaning on the handle of the axe, the head resting on the chopping block. "I was wondering when I'd see you. I hear your princess is likely to go mad."

"Why would people be saying that?"

"Either that or she'll die."

"What!" Ruairidh stared at the man as if he was the one who'd gone mad.

"The lake is sinking. Some say it's because the princess has forsaken it, others that she's gone into a decline because it's sinking."

"Surely the lake will fill again when your rainy season starts."

Ailig shook his head. "We have no rainy season. The lake has always filled from springs and streams. They've all dried up. It's the first time that anyone can recall this happening. The lake is sinking and it'll soon be dry. People say it's the witch again, but she denies it."

"Someone has to be able to do something. What about the king? Isn't he worried about his daughter?"

"Of course he is. But what can he do? He sent out a proclamation that he'd handsomely reward anyone who could solve the problem, but no one's come forward. Do you know how to make springs bubble up again?"

"No. But there has to be something." He tried to think of what could be done. He drew a blank. Moire must be frantic. She lived for her moments in the lake. And not only that, she wasn't herself when she was on the land.

Ailig shrugged. "There's a hermit up in the hills you could see. The wisest man I know of. But you might want to go soon. They say she just lies there, fading away like the lake. Hasn't even shed a tear. You'd think she'd at least shed a tear. But she doesn't laugh anymore either. Now everyone thought that'd be a good thing with how she laughed at even misfortune, but I hear it's a sadder thing that she doesn't laugh at all."

He had to do something. He couldn't let her fade away with the lake. "Can you tell me where to find the hermit?"

"I'll draw you a map."

When Ruairidh had the map tucked away in his coin purse, he headed for the castle. He needed to see for himself how Moire was before he went looking for the hermit. Knowing that after months of living in a cave he no longer looked like a prince, he sought out the lord chamberlain and asked if he might be allowed to tend the princess by cleaning her shoes. The lord chamberlain finally agreed and Ruairidh spent the next week trying to catch a glimpse of Moire. It was impossible. She didn't leave her room. Ever. The closest he could get to her was polishing her unworn boots.

While he spent the week trying to see the princess, the lake continued to dry, fish dying in the sun, large areas of cracked earth left behind once the mud hardened. Unable to see the princess, worried and not knowing what to do, he pulled out Ailig's map and decided to try and find the hermit.

The journey to the hermit took longer than he planned and Ruairidh called into Ailig to let him know the hermit hadn't been able to help. Ailig rushed to meet him.

"Ruairidh, I was wondering when you'd return. There's been news. Not very good news, but news all the same."

"Has the lake started to fill?"

"No, I'm afraid not. But a group of boys playing in the last of the deep holes found a golden plate engraved with what must be done to fill the lake again."

Relief filled him. "That's good because the hermit wasn't able to help."

"No, I'm afraid it isn't good. It's a hopeless cause. No one would ever follow the instructions. The lake will soon be completely dry and no one will stop it."

"What do the words say?"

"That the hole the lake drains through can only be filled by the body of a living and willing man. The king offered an enormous reward, but not a single man has come forward. Not that I blame them. Who wants to die a slow death? It'd take a day for the lake to refill once the hole is plugged. Spending an entire day waiting for death-" Ailig broke off and shook his head. "I don't know a single man who could manage it."

"Are you certain?"

"You can see the king's proclamation if you go into town, but I have to warn you that several of your companions have stayed there in the hope you'll turn up."

"Moire will die if no one does anything about the lake."

"There you have it. Someone's sure to die before much longer. Not that she'd ever mourn the man who'd sacrifice himself to save her. She's too empty headed for that."

Ruairidh thought of the young woman who'd swum with him of an evening. That woman wasn't empty headed. The princess that was to be found on the land was not the one that could be found in the water. "Thank you, Ailig." He reached out to momentarily rest a hand on the man's shoulder, still uncertain if he could go through with it. "Take care of my horse."

"You're not going to sacrifice yourself are you? You're far better than The Light Princess."

Ruairidh thought of the many princesses he'd met in his search for a bride. No, there wasn't another woman like his Moire. He thought of spending his life with one of those many women and shuddered. A lifetime without his own princess would be hell. "Tell my companions in a few days." He held out his hand. "And thank you for all the help you've given me."

Ailig shook his hand. "You're mad."

Ruairidh grinned. "A mad man for a mad princess. Sounds about right to me." He took out his coin purse and gave it to Ailig. He wouldn't need it.

"May the end be swift and painless."

Ruairidh strode away, glancing back before he stepped into the trees, finding that Ailig stared after him. He forced himself to return to the castle, reminding himself it was the only way to save Moire.

Asking around he learned the king was in his counting house where he was told that it was unwise to ever disturb him. Ignoring the advice he knocked on the door, swinging it open. The king leapt from his seat, knocking over a pile of gold coins as he drew his sword.

"Please Your Majesty, I have come to offer my services to repair your lake."

"You've come to do what?"

"I will sacrifice myself to repair the lake."

"Are you mad?"

"Does it matter?"

The king sheathed his sword. "I suppose it doesn't. What do you want me to do with the reward?"

"I don't want the reward you offered. I have a different request."

"Never. Do you think you can bleed me dry for the sake of your miserable life?" The king drew his sword again. "You'll take what I'm willing to offer and be grateful, wretch."

"Then I won't be helping you."

"I'll make you fix the lake."

"You need a willing man. Unless you agree to my condition, I won't go willingly. It's such a small condition."

"Then what is it?"

Ruairidh took a deep breath, surprised to find he was trembling. "Since I must wait many hours before I die, I ask only that your daughter, the princess, shall stay with me. That she will feed me with her own hands and look at me now and then to comfort me. As soon as the water is up to my eyes, she may go." His voice faltered on the last three words and he swallowed hard, pushing thoughts of his death from his mind. He could do this. He must do this. There was no other way to save Moire.

"Why didn't you tell me before

what your condition was? Such a fuss about nothing!" The king sheathed his sword again. "Would you like to run and see your parents before you attempt to save the lake?"

He thought of his parents when they finally learned of what had happened to him and hoped that his younger brother was a better son to them. "No, thank you."

"Then I'll send my people to look for the hole at once."

By morning the hole had been found. Moire was laid in one of the little boats in a bed of pillows, a canopy erected over it and ribbons keeping her from floating away. Ruairidh was dressed in some borrowed finery. If he was to die it would be dressed like the prince he was. Several attendants helped him into the hole. He put both his legs in, sitting on a rock that was by the edge of the hole. He then leaned forward and covered the rest of the hole with his hands.

The water stopped draining away. He momentarily closed his eyes. The writing on the gold plate looked to be true. Already he could feel the water had risen a little higher. "You may go," he told the attendants.

They looked to the princess who had sat up from her bed of pillows to watch the proceedings. At a nod from her, they left.

When the princess lay back down on her pillows, with barely another glance in his direction, he tried to think of a way to catch her attention. He thought of the song he'd sung to her ages ago. Maybe she'd remember it. When he was partway through the song, she sat up and watched him.

Curiosity in her eyes, but no recognition. He fell silent when he reached the end of the song.

"Another one. Sing more," Moire ordered.

He couldn't. He'd noticed how much the water had risen and how it now lapped around the boat which had been resting in mud.

"If you don't know another, sing it again. It makes the waiting less tedious."

He tried to remind himself that she wasn't herself. That out of the water she was a different person, but her words still hurt.

Moire stared at him a moment longer. "You bringing my lake back, it's very kind." She closed her eyes, lying back down on her pillows.

Still he couldn't bring himself to speak, afraid he might instead beg to be released. She was worth dying for. The woman she became when she was in the water, that woman was worth dying for.

Hours passed and he began to wish there was a canopy over him like the one that had been erected above the boat Moire lay in. Not once did she rise and check on him and he became annoyed. Surely even when she wasn't herself she must understand what he was doing for her. What it meant for him. "Princess!" His voice was sharper than he'd planned it to be.

She sat up, looking at the water instead of Ruairidh. "I'm afloat. Oh look at how much the water has risen. My lake is coming back."

"Princess." Was it too much to ask for a little of her attention?

"Well?" Still her gaze remained on the water.

"Your father promised that you'd look at me."

"Did he? Then I suppose I must. But I'm so sleepy."

"Sleep, then. Don't mind me." His heart sank. A moment with his princess would have been perfect, but the spell she was under was too strong when she wasn't in the lake.

"I think I will sleep again."

"Before you do, could you give me a glass of wine and a biscuit first?"

Moire yawned, pouring a glass of wine and taking a biscuit from the basket of food in her boat. Leaning over the side of the boat towards him, she stared at him. "You don't look well. Are you sure you don't mind being down there?"

He tried to control the flare of

anger her words caused. Of course he didn't look well. Taking a calming breath he reminded himself of the spell. "I am fine, only I'll die before I'm of any use to you, unless I have something to eat."

"Here then." She held out the wine and biscuit to him.

"You must feed me. I dare not move my hands. The water would run away if I did."

"Oh, we don't want that." Moire broke off bits of biscuit and fed him, offering him sips of wine.

As she fed him, he kissed the tips of her fingers, but she didn't seem to notice. A single moment with his Moire. Just one moment, that was all he wanted. But it looked like his wish would remain unfilled. Instead his last moments would be spent with The Light Princess.

Once the wine had been drunk and the biscuit eaten, she started to lie back down.

"Please don't go to sleep. You must sit and look at me and help me stay awake. I wouldn't want to fall asleep and let the water out of the lake."

"If I must." She made herself comfortable and sat staring at him.

The sun went down, and the moon rose and the water continued to rise up around Ruairidh's body. It was up to his waist now. He stared at her, memorising every inch of her face, wanting to take the image with him when the water finally covered his head.

"Why can't we have a swim?" Moire asked. "There seems water enough for a swim."

"I shall never swim again."

"Oh, I forgot." She fell silent, staring at him as he'd requested.

The water continued to rise and the night grew later. Moire occasionally fed Ruairidh and watched him like he'd asked. When the water rose to his neck, he asked her for a kiss.

"If you wish." She leaned forward and pressed her lips to his.

He'd lost feeling in most of his body and was glad of it, otherwise he didn't know if he could have continued to remain in the hole as the water rose. He tried to keep his thoughts on the kiss, but it was hard when death was so close. The water continued to rise. It touched his chin.

"I remember you. We fell into the lake together. It was great fun." She frowned. "I'd like to do that again." The water rose over his lips and

Moire pulled herself into the water, using the side of the boat. Her mouth opened and shock filled her eyes. "No! Oh Ruairidh, no." She reached for him tugging at his body.

Water covered his face and he stared through it at her, wishing he could tell her not to be scared. She'd have her lake and be herself again. But she continued to tug frantically at him. He couldn't watch her anymore and closed his eyes. There was nothing she could do. He felt his hands pulled from the hole then first one leg and then the other. He was dragged into the boat and water droplets fell upon him as he struggled to breathe. Opening his eyes he saw it wasn't water droplets, it was tears.

Moire cried, her tears raining over him as she called his name, shaking his body when he didn't answer. She was his last image before the world went black.

When Ruairidh came to, lying in a bed, it was to see Moire's profile as she glared at the chamberlain who stood in front of her with his nightcap on.

"But Princess, what about the lake?"

"Go and drown yourself in it, but get out of my sight."

Ruairidh laughed softly as the man scurried away.

Moire dropped down beside him, clutching at his shoulders, tears still streaming down her cheeks. "Oh Ruairidh, how could I have survived if you'd died?"

He felt the weight of her hands against his shoulders and lifted one, seeing blisters on her palms.

She pulled her hand away from him, closing it. "I had to row you back to shore. My hands are a mess, but you'll be fine, won't you?"

He took her hand again. "You have your gravity. You're out of the water and you still have your gravity."

"And I'm none too happy about that. Do you know how hard it is to walk? I'm barely able to sit and rise. Walking is a nightmare. It was a good thing my attendants waited on the shore for me or I'd never have been able to get you to the castle."

"Why are you crying?" He ran a finger down her cheek.

"I can't seem to stop."

"And the lake?"

She smiled through her tears. "It's raining and the lake is continuing to rise."

Ruairidh grinned. "I was worried all those hours I spent blocking the hole were for nothing."

"Forget the lake. How could you have even thought I'd prefer a lake to you?"

He laughed, drawing her close. "The spell is broken. You're on land and yet you're still you." He tried to hold back the words that he'd wanted to speak for so long, but it was impossible. "Moire, will you marry me?"

Her laughter filled the room. "And everyone says that I'm the one who's inappropriate. Couldn't you have waited until you were well and I'd learned to walk so we could do it properly?"

"Not at all."

Still grinning, she nodded. "I'm glad."

"So what is your answer?"

"Of course it is yes, you stupid man."

Before Ruairidh could reminisce about the first day they'd met, a servant burst into the room.

"Your Highness, we've just had news. Princess Makemnoit's house has collapsed in upon itself and there's now a stream leading from it to the lake. I'm afraid she was in her house when it happened. We think it's from all this rain we're having. We've never seen the like of it before."

Ruairidh was relieved. Maybe she hadn't been the one to bewitch Moire, but most people thought she had. Now she wouldn't have the chance to ever bewitch anyone again. He thought of Ailig, his entourage still searching for him, and his parents. He'd have to send news to each of them about his own whereabouts. But for now he had other things to focus on.

"You may go," Moire said to the servant.

"But Your-" the servant began.

"Go." Moire's tone was sharp and the servant scurried away. "Now where were we?" Her tone softened and she smiled.

"I believe we were talking about the future." The future. How good that word sounded.

"No, I believe the talking was done and you were about to seal our betrothal."

Ruairidh laughed. His arms tightened around her as his lips met hers. It was far better than the kiss he'd shared with her while she'd still been under the spell. This time she had her gravity and didn't feel like she'd float away at any moment and be lost to him forever. Now she felt like she'd stay.

Free Ebook

Subscribe to Avril's newsletter and receive a free ebook. This ebook is exclusive to those on her mailing list. To find out more about this offer visit:

www.avrilsabine.com/free-ebook

*

We value your privacy and will not sell, rent, exchange or loan your email address to third parties. Your information is confidential and you are under no obligation to remain on the mailing list and can unsubscribe at any time.

To The Reader

If you enjoyed this book, why not consider leaving a review to help other readers discover it too? Reader engagement is one of the few ways that lets an author know readers want more books in a particular series or genre. So leave a review and tell friends, not only about this book but also about other ones you've enjoyed, so you can continue to enjoy books by your favourite authors for years to come.

Dreams are meant to be lived,

Avril.

About The Author

Avril is an Australian author who lives with her family on acreage in South East Queensland. She writes mostly young adult and children's speculative fiction, but has been known to dabble in other genres. You can find more information about her at www.avrilsabine.com where you can also subscribe to her newsletter to be kept informed about new releases, current projects, blog posts and exclusive news.

Titles By Avril Sabine

Stories about strong characters and characters who discover their strengths.

SERIES

Assassins Of The Dead- Young Adult Fantasy/Paranormal

Book 1: Dark Blade

Book 2: Dragon Touched

Book 3: Society Against Vampires

Book 4: King's Request

Dragon Blood- Young Adult Urban Fantasy (with elements of romance)

(5 book series)

Book 1: Pliethin

Book 2: Wyvern

Book 3: Surety

Book 4: Knight

Book 5: Mage

Dragon Mage- Young Adult Urban Fantasy (with elements of romance)

(Series two of Dragon Blood series)

Book 1: Promise

Dragon Blood Chronicles- Young Adult Urban Fantasy (with elements of romance)

(Companion stand alone series to Dragon Blood)

Book 1: Oath

Book 2: Betrayed

Guardians Of The Round Table- Young Adult Fantasy LitRPG

(Co-written with Storm and Rhys Petersen)

Book 1: Dexterity Fail

Book 2: Goblin Boots

Book 3: Singed Feathers

Book 4: Frog Mage

Book 5: Crystal Mine

Book 6: Cursed Harp

Book 7: Treasure Seeker

Rosie's Rangers- Young Adult Western Steampunk

(6 book series)

Book 1: Justice

Book 2: Vengeance

Book 3: Treachery

Book 4: Accused

Book 5: Wanted

Book 6: Corruption

Mark Of Kings- Children's Fantasy

(Upper middle grade/preteen)

(4 book series)

Book 1: The Arena

Book 2: The Island

Book 3: The Assassin

Book 4: The King

STAND ALONE SERIES

Demon Hunters- Young Adult Urban Fantasy/Horror (with elements of romance)

Book 1: Blood Sacrifice

Book 2: Retribution

Book 3: Tainted

Book 4: Premonition

Book 5: Cursed

Book 6: Feud

Book 7: Extrication

Plea Of The Damned- Young Adult Urban Fantasy/Paranormal

(6 book series)

Book 1: Forgive Me Lucy

Book 2: Forgive Me Aiden

Book 3: Forgive Me Jena

Book 4: Forgive Me Kobe

Book 5: Forgive Me Marti

Book 6: Forgive Me Dawson

Realms Of The Fae- Young Adult Urban Fantasy (with elements of romance)

The Sword (short story in Like A Girl Anthology)

Heart Of Stone

Book 1: A Debt Owed

Book 2: Marked By The Hunt

Book 3: The Magic Collector

Book 4: An Unexpected Betrayal

Book 5: Imprisoned By Iron

Fairytales Retold (Short Stories)

Snow-White And Rose-Red

The Twelve Brothers

The Light Princess

Beauty And The Beast

Sleeping Beauty

Aschenputtel

The Golden Bird

The Frog Prince

The Death Of Koshchei The Deathless

Myths And Legends Retold (Short Stories)

Ion, Son Of Apollo

Sir Gawain And The Maid With The Narrow Sleeves

Princess Ilse, The Giant's Daughter

YOUNG ADULT NOVELS

Young Adult Fantasy (with elements of romance)

Elf Sight

Earth Bound

Young Adult Urban Fantasy

Stone Warrior (with elements of romance)

The Jungle Inside

Young Adult Contemporary (with elements of romance)

Through Your Eyes

The Ugly Stepsister

Perfect Little Princess

Young Adult Contemporary/ Paranormal

Whispers In The Dark (with elements of romance and same sex relationships)

Over Too Soon (with elements of romance)

Young Adult Sci-Fi

Experiment X-One-Six (Urban Sci-Fi/Superheroes)

An Endless Dawn (Post Apocalyptic Sci-Fi)

CHILDREN'S BOOKS

Dragon Lord (Preteen/early teens) (Fantasy)

The Irish Wizard (Upper middle grade) (Urban Fantasy)

SHORT STORIES

Urban Fantasy

Eternally Late

Dealings With Joe

Glimpses (short story in That Moment When Anthology)

Contemporary

The Brat Next Door

Fantasy LitRPG

(Set in the same world as Guardians Of The Round Table Series)

Tales Of Inadon 1: The Disc (Co-written with Storm and Rhys Petersen) (short story in Game On! Anthology)

Post Apocalyptic Sci-Fi

Compulsive Directive

NONFICTION

A Year Of Weekly Writing Exercises (Creative Writing)

Cooking For Families With Allergies (Cooking) (Co-written with Storm Petersen)

Tell Me A Story, Grandma (Memoir)

For the most up to date details on available titles visit:

www.avrilsabine.com/books/bibliography

Disclaimer

This is a work of fiction. Names, characters, businesses, places, events and incidents are either the products of the author's imagination or used in a fictitious manner. Any resemblance to actual persons, living or dead, or actual events is purely coincidental. The opinions expressed or beliefs held are those of the characters and should not be assumed to be the opinions or beliefs of the author.

www.ingramcontent.com/pod-product-compliance
Lightning Source LLC
Chambersburg PA
CBHW020821190726
48285CB00006B/2360